Tables, Numbers & more...

12 × 6 = 72

Name ______________________

Class ______________ Sec. __________

School ______________________

____

19 × 2 = 38

16 × 8 = 128

LITTLE SCHOLARZ PVT LTD.

This Book first originated and published in 2017 by

LITTLE SCHOLARZ PVT LTD.

12 - H, New Daryaganj Road, Opp. Officers' Mess, New Delhi - 110002 (India)
Phone # 91-11-23275124, 23275224, 23245124, 23261567
email - sales@littlescholarz.com
website - www.littlescholarz.com

Tables, Numbers & more ...

ISBN : 978-93-86063-22-9
Book Code : S-412

Tables 1 to 3

1 × 1 = 1	2 × 1 = 2	3 × 1 = 3
1 × 2 = 2	2 × 2 = 4	3 × 2 = 6
1 × 3 = 3	2 × 3 = 6	3 × 3 = 9
1 × 4 = 4	2 × 4 = 8	3 × 4 = 12
1 × 5 = 5	2 × 5 = 10	3 × 5 = 15
1 × 6 = 6	2 × 6 = 12	3 × 6 = 18
1 × 7 = 7	2 × 7 = 14	3 × 7 = 21
1 × 8 = 8	2 × 8 = 16	3 × 8 = 24
1 × 9 = 9	2 × 9 = 18	3 × 9 = 27
1 × 10 = 10	2 × 10 = 20	3 × 10 = 30

Tables 4 to 6

4 × 1 = 4	5 × 1 = 5	6 × 1 = 6
4 × 2 = 8	5 × 2 = 10	6 × 2 = 12
4 × 3 = 12	5 × 3 = 15	6 × 3 = 18
4 × 4 = 16	5 × 4 = 20	6 × 4 = 24
4 × 5 = 20	5 × 5 = 25	6 × 5 = 30
4 × 6 = 24	5 × 6 = 30	6 × 6 = 36
4 × 7 = 28	5 × 7 = 35	6 × 7 = 42
4 × 8 = 32	5 × 8 = 40	6 × 8 = 48
4 × 9 = 36	5 × 9 = 45	6 × 9 = 54
4 × 10 = 40	5 × 10 = 50	6 × 10 = 60

Tables 7 to 9

7 × 1 = 7	8 × 1 = 8	9 × 1 = 9
7 × 2 = 14	8 × 2 = 16	9 × 2 = 18
7 × 3 = 21	8 × 3 = 24	9 × 3 = 27
7 × 4 = 28	8 × 4 = 32	9 × 4 = 36
7 × 5 = 35	8 × 5 = 40	9 × 5 = 45
7 × 6 = 42	8 × 6 = 48	9 × 6 = 54
7 × 7 = 49	8 × 7 = 56	9 × 7 = 63
7 × 8 = 56	8 × 8 = 64	9 × 8 = 72
7 × 9 = 63	8 × 9 = 72	9 × 9 = 81
7 × 10 = 70	8 × 10 = 80	9 × 10 = 90

Tables 10 to 12

Table of 10	Table of 11	Table of 12
10 × 1 = 10	11 × 1 = 11	12 × 1 = 12
10 × 2 = 20	11 × 2 = 22	12 × 2 = 24
10 × 3 = 30	11 × 3 = 33	12 × 3 = 36
10 × 4 = 40	11 × 4 = 44	12 × 4 = 48
10 × 5 = 50	11 × 5 = 55	12 × 5 = 60
10 × 6 = 60	11 × 6 = 66	12 × 6 = 72
10 × 7 = 70	11 × 7 = 77	12 × 7 = 84
10 × 8 = 80	11 × 8 = 88	12 × 8 = 96
10 × 9 = 90	11 × 9 = 99	12 × 9 = 108
10 × 10 = 100	11 × 10 = 110	12 × 10 = 120

Tables 13 to 15

13 × 1 = 13	14 × 1 = 14	15 × 1 = 15
13 × 2 = 26	14 × 2 = 28	15 × 2 = 30
13 × 3 = 39	14 × 3 = 42	15 × 3 = 45
13 × 4 = 52	14 × 4 = 56	15 × 4 = 60
13 × 5 = 65	14 × 5 = 70	15 × 5 = 75
13 × 6 = 78	14 × 6 = 84	15 × 6 = 90
13 × 7 = 91	14 × 7 = 98	15 × 7 = 105
13 × 8 = 104	14 × 8 = 112	15 × 8 = 120
13 × 9 = 117	14 × 9 = 126	15 × 9 = 135
13 × 10 = 130	14 × 10 = 140	15 × 10 = 150

Tables 16 to 18

16 × 1 = 16	17 × 1 = 17	18 × 1 = 18
16 × 2 = 32	17 × 2 = 34	18 × 2 = 36
16 × 3 = 48	17 × 3 = 51	18 × 3 = 54
16 × 4 = 64	17 × 4 = 68	18 × 4 = 72
16 × 5 = 80	17 × 5 = 85	18 × 5 = 90
16 × 6 = 96	17 × 6 = 102	18 × 6 = 108
16 × 7 = 112	17 × 7 = 119	18 × 7 = 126
16 × 8 = 128	17 × 8 = 136	18 × 8 = 144
16 × 9 = 144	17 × 9 = 153	18 × 9 = 162
16 × 10 = 160	17 × 10 = 170	18 × 10 = 180

Tables 19 to 21

19 × 1 = 19	20 × 1 = 20	21 × 1 = 21
19 × 2 = 38	20 × 2 = 40	21 × 2 = 42
19 × 3 = 57	20 × 3 = 60	21 × 3 = 63
19 × 4 = 76	20 × 4 = 80	21 × 4 = 84
19 × 5 = 95	20 × 5 = 100	21 × 5 = 105
19 × 6 = 114	20 × 6 = 120	21 × 6 = 126
19 × 7 = 133	20 × 7 = 140	21 × 7 = 147
19 × 8 = 152	20 × 8 = 160	21 × 8 = 168
19 × 9 = 171	20 × 9 = 180	21 × 9 = 189
19 × 10 = 190	20 × 10 = 200	21 × 10 = 210

Tables 22 to 24

22 × 1 = 22	23 × 1 = 23	24 × 1 = 24
22 × 2 = 44	23 × 2 = 46	24 × 2 = 48
22 × 3 = 66	23 × 3 = 69	24 × 3 = 72
22 × 4 = 88	23 × 4 = 92	24 × 4 = 96
22 × 5 = 110	23 × 5 = 115	24 × 5 = 120
22 × 6 = 132	23 × 6 = 138	24 × 6 = 144
22 × 7 = 154	23 × 7 = 161	24 × 7 = 168
22 × 8 = 176	23 × 8 = 184	24 × 8 = 192
22 × 9 = 198	23 × 9 = 207	24 × 9 = 216
22 × 10 = 220	23 × 10 = 230	24 × 10 = 240

Tables 25 to 27

25 × 1 = 25	26 × 1 = 26	27 × 1 = 27
25 × 2 = 50	26 × 2 = 52	27 × 2 = 54
25 × 3 = 75	26 × 3 = 78	27 × 3 = 81
25 × 4 = 100	26 × 4 = 104	27 × 4 = 108
25 × 5 = 125	26 × 5 = 130	27 × 5 = 135
25 × 6 = 150	26 × 6 = 156	27 × 6 = 162
25 × 7 = 175	26 × 7 = 182	27 × 7 = 189
25 × 8 = 200	26 × 8 = 208	27 × 8 = 216
25 × 9 = 225	26 × 9 = 234	27 × 9 = 243
25 × 10 = 250	26 × 10 = 260	27 × 10 = 270

Tables 28 to 30

28 × 1 = 28	29 × 1 = 29	30 × 1 = 30
28 × 2 = 56	29 × 2 = 58	30 × 2 = 60
28 × 3 = 84	29 × 3 = 87	30 × 3 = 90
28 × 4 = 112	29 × 4 = 116	30 × 4 = 120
28 × 5 = 140	29 × 5 = 145	30 × 5 = 150
28 × 6 = 168	29 × 6 = 174	30 × 6 = 180
28 × 7 = 196	29 × 7 = 203	30 × 7 = 210
28 × 8 = 224	29 × 8 = 232	30 × 8 = 240
28 × 9 = 252	29 × 9 = 261	30 × 9 = 270
28 × 10 = 280	29 × 10 = 290	30 × 10 = 300

Tables 31 to 33

31 × 1 = 31	32 × 1 = 32	33 × 1 = 33
31 × 2 = 62	32 × 2 = 64	33 × 2 = 66
31 × 3 = 93	32 × 3 = 96	33 × 3 = 99
31 × 4 = 124	32 × 4 = 128	33 × 4 = 132
31 × 5 = 155	32 × 5 = 160	33 × 5 = 165
31 × 6 = 186	32 × 6 = 192	33 × 6 = 198
31 × 7 = 217	32 × 7 = 224	33 × 7 = 231
31 × 8 = 248	32 × 8 = 256	33 × 8 = 264
31 × 9 = 279	32 × 9 = 288	33 × 9 = 297
31 × 10 = 310	32 × 10 = 320	33 × 10 = 330

Tables 34 to 36

34 × 1 = 34	35 × 1 = 35	36 × 1 = 36
34 × 2 = 68	35 × 2 = 70	36 × 2 = 72
34 × 3 = 102	35 × 3 = 105	36 × 3 = 108
34 × 4 = 136	35 × 4 = 140	36 × 4 = 144
34 × 5 = 170	35 × 5 = 175	36 × 5 = 180
34 × 6 = 204	35 × 6 = 210	36 × 6 = 216
34 × 7 = 238	35 × 7 = 245	36 × 7 = 252
34 × 8 = 272	35 × 8 = 280	36 × 8 = 288
34 × 9 = 306	35 × 9 = 315	36 × 9 = 324
34 × 10 = 340	35 × 10 = 350	36 × 10 = 360

Tables 37 to 40

37 × 1 = 37	38 × 1 = 38	39 × 1 = 39	40 × 1 = 40
37 × 2 = 74	38 × 2 = 76	39 × 2 = 78	40 × 2 = 80
37 × 3 = 111	38 × 3 = 114	39 × 3 = 117	40 × 3 = 120
37 × 4 = 148	38 × 4 = 152	39 × 4 = 156	40 × 4 = 160
37 × 5 = 185	38 × 5 = 190	39 × 5 = 195	40 × 5 = 200
37 × 6 = 222	38 × 6 = 228	39 × 6 = 234	40 × 6 = 240
37 × 7 = 259	38 × 7 = 266	39 × 7 = 273	40 × 7 = 280
37 × 8 = 296	38 × 8 = 304	39 × 8 = 312	40 × 8 = 320
37 × 9 = 333	38 × 9 = 342	39 × 9 = 351	40 × 9 = 360
37 × 10 = 370	38 × 10 = 380	39 × 10 = 390	40 × 10 = 400

Numbers with their Different Expressions

Arabic Numerals*	Cardinal Numbers	Roman Numerals	Arabic Numerals	Cardinal Numbers	Roman Numerals
1	One	I	28	Twenty eight	XXVIII
2	Two	II	29	Twenty nine	XXIX
3	Three	III	30	Thirty	XXX
4	Four	IV	31	Thirty one	XXXI
5	Five	V	32	Thirty two	XXXII
6	Six	VI	33	Thirty three	XXXIII
7	Seven	VII	34	Thirty four	XXXIV
8	Eight	VIII	35	Thirty five	XXXV
9	Nine	IX	36	Thirty six	XXXVI
10	Ten	X	37	Thirty seven	XXXVII
11	Eleven	XI	38	Thirty eight	XXXVIII
12	Twelve	XII	39	Thirty nine	XXXIX
13	Thirteen	XIII	40	Forty	XL
14	Fourteen	XIV	41	Forty one	XLI
15	Fifteen	XV	42	Forty two	XLII
16	Sixteen	XVI	43	Forty three	XLIII
17	Seventeen	XVII	44	Forty four	XLIV
18	Eighteen	XVIII	45	Forty five	XLV
19	Nineteen	XIX	46	Forty six	XLVI
20	Twenty	XX	47	Forty seven	XLVII
21	Twenty one	XXI	48	Forty eight	XLVIII
22	Twenty two	XXII	49	Forty nine	XLIX
23	Twenty three	XXIII	50	Fifty	L
24	Twenty four	XXIV	51	Fifty one	LI
25	Twenty five	XXV	52	Fifty two	LII
26	Twenty six	XXVI	53	Fifty three	LIII
27	Twenty seven	XXVII	54	Fifty four	LIV

*Also known as Hindu-Arabic Numerals OR Hindu Numerals.

Arabic Numerals	Cardinal Numbers	Roman Numerals
55	Fifty five	LV
56	Fifty six	LVI
57	Fifty seven	LVII
58	Fifty eight	LVIII
59	Fifty nine	LIX
60	Sixty	LX
61	Sixty one	LXI
62	Sixty two	LXII
63	Sixty three	LXIII
64	Sixty four	LXIV
65	Sixty five	LXV
66	Sixty six	LXVI
67	Sixty seven	LXVII
68	Sixty eight	LXVIII
69	Sixty nine	LXIX
70	Seventy	LXX
71	Seventy one	LXXI
72	Seventy two	LXXII
73	Seventy three	LXXIII
74	Seventy four	LXXIV
75	Seventy five	LXXV
76	Seventy six	LXXVI
77	Seventy seven	LXXVII
78	Seventy eight	LXXVIII
79	Seventy nine	LXXIX
80	Eighty	LXXX
81	Eighty one	LXXXI
82	Eighty two	LXXXII
83	Eighty three	LXXXIII

Arabic Numerals	Cardinal Numbers	Roman Numerals
84	Eighty four	LXXXIV
85	Eighty five	LXXXV
86	Eighty six	LXXXVI
87	Eighty seven	LXXXVII
88	Eighty eight	LXXXVIII
89	Eighty nine	LXXXIX
90	Ninety	XC
91	Ninety one	XCI
92	Ninety two	XCII
93	Ninety three	XCIII
94	Ninety four	XCIV
95	Ninety five	XCV
96	Ninety six	XCVI
97	Ninety seven	XCVII
98	Ninety eight	XCVIII
99	Ninety nine	XCIX
100	Hundred	C

Bigger Numbers with their Expressions

200	Two-hundred	CC
300	Three-hundred	CCC
400	Four-hundred	CD
500	Five-hundred	D
600	Six-hundred	DC
700	Seven-hundred	DCC
800	Eight-hundred	DCCC
900	Nine-hundred	CM
1000	One-thousand	M

The Number System

Whole Numbers:

Whole Numbers are simply the numbers from: 0, 1, 2, 3, 4, 5..........

Counting Numbers:

Counting Numbers are Whole Numbers but without zero: 1, 2, 3,.....

Natural Numbers:

Natural Numbers are Counting Numbers: 1, 2, 3, 4,........

The number 0 is a Whole number. Sometimes 0 is also included in Natural Numbers making them look like Whole Numbers.

Even and Odd Numbers

Even Numbers:

The numbers which are exactly divisible by 2 are called Even Numbers.

They are: 2, 4, 6, 8, 10, ... etc.

Even numbers have digits: 0, 2, 4, 6 or 8 at their one's place.

Odd Numbers:

The numbers which are not exactly divisible by 2 are called Odd Numbers.

They are: 1, 3, 5, 7, 9, 11, 13, 15, ... etc.

A number can either be Even or Odd, it can never be both.

While counting from 1 every odd number is followed by an even number and vice-versa.

Prime and Composite Numbers

Prime Numbers

A number which is divisible by 1 and itself only, is called Prime Number. It is never divisible by any other number. The following are the Prime numbers between 1 and 100:

2, 3, 5, 7, 11, 13, 17, 19, 23, 29, 31, 37, 41, 43, 47, 53, 59, 61, 67, 71, 73, 79, 83, 89, 97.

There are 25 Prime Numbers between 1 to 100.

2 is the smallest Prime Number. Every Prime Number except 2, is an odd number.

Composite Numbers

The numbers which can be divided evenly by numbers other than themselves and 1, are called Composite Numbers.

The following are the Composite numbers from 1 to 100: 4, 6, 8, 9, 10, 12, 14, 15, 16, 18, 20, 21, 22, 24, 25, 26, 27, 28, 30, 32, 33, 34, 35, 36, 38, 39, 40, 42, 44, 45, 46, 48, 49, 50, 51, 52, 54, 55, 56, 57, 58, 60, 62, 63, 64, 65, 66, 68, 69, 70, 72, 74, 75, 76, 77, 78, 80, 81, 82, 84, 85, 86, 87, 88, 90, 91, 92, 93, 94, 95, 96, 98, 99, 100.

The Smallest Composite Number is 4.

A number can either be a Prime or a Composite number, it can never be both.

1 is neither a Prime nor a Composite Number.

Factors and Multiples

Factors

A factor of a number is an exact divisor of that number.
e.g., 1, 2, 3 and 6 are the factors of 6.

- The Number 1 is a factor of every number.
- Every number is a factor of itself.
- Every Factor is less than or equal to the given number.

Multiples

A number is a multiple of its each factor. *e.g.,* 8 is the multiple of 1, 2, 4 and 8.

- Every Number is a multiple of itself.
- Every multiple of a number is greater than or equal to that number.

Prime Factor

A prime number which is the factor of another number, is called a prime factor.
e.g., 3 is the prime factor of 9.

Geometrical Shapes

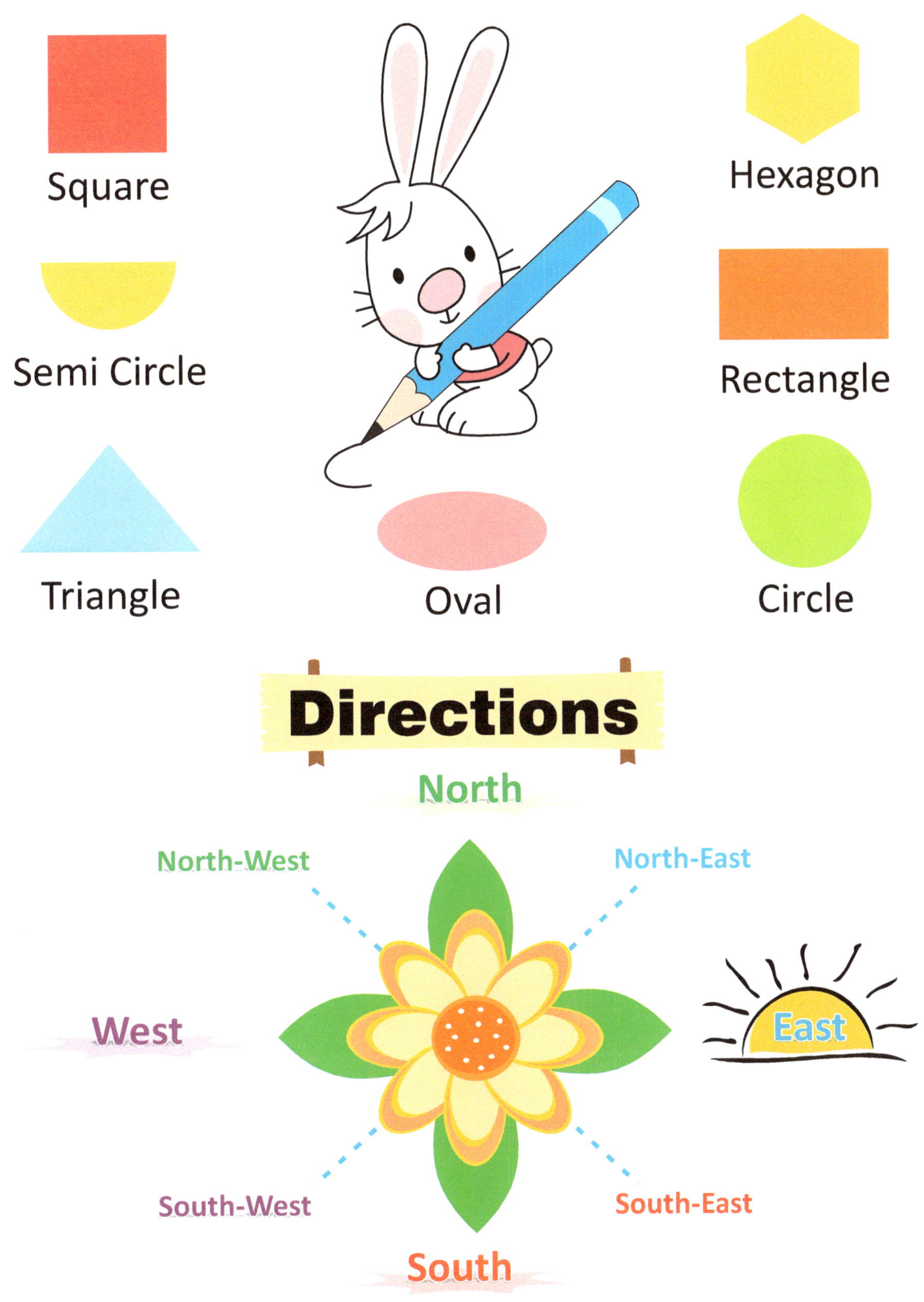

Directions

Tests of Divisibility

Divisible by 2:

A number is divisible by 2 if its last digit is even or zero *e.g.* 548, 724, 1080 etc. are all divisible by 2.

Divisible by 3:

A number is divisible by 3 if the sum of its digits is divisible by 3, *e.g.* 18, 51, 60 etc. are all divisible by 3.

The number 153 = 1 + 5 + 3 = 9
The number 1986 = 1 + 9 + 8 + 6 = 24

Divisible by 4:

A number is divisible by 4 if the number formed by its last two digits is divisible by 4, *e.g.* 24, 44, 52 etc.

12 16 20 24 48 72

Divisible by 5:

A number is divisible by 5 if its last digit is 0 or 5, *e.g.* 5, 20, 45, 100 etc.

10 15 20 25 35 45 60

Divisible by 6:

A number is divisible by 6 if it is divisible by both 2 and 3, *e.g.* 18, 36, 72 etc.

12 24 18 36 48 60 72

Divisible by 7:

A number is divisible by 7 if the difference between twice the digit in its unit's place and the number formed by other digits is either 0 or a multiple of 7. *e.g.,*

The Number 217 has last digit = 7
Twice last digit = $2 \times 7 = 14$
Number formed by other digits = 21
Difference = $21 - 14 = 7$
$\therefore$ 217 is divisible by 7.

Divisible by 8:

A number is divisible by 8 if number formed by its last three digits is divisible by 8. *e.g.,*

The number 60432 has last 3 digits = 432
Which is divisible by 8
$\therefore$ 60432 is divisible by 8.

Divisible by 9:

A number is divisible by 9 if the sum of its digit is divisible by 9, *e.g.* 27, 81, 108 etc.

The number 1674 = $1 + 6 + 7 + 4 = 18$
Which is divisible by 9.

Divisible by 10:

A number is divisible by 10, if its last digit is 0, *e.g.* 20, 40, 100 etc.

- If two numbers are divisible by a number, then their sum will also be divisible by that number. *e.g.,* 16 and 20 are both divisible by 4. Their sum $16 + 20 = 36$ is also divisible by 4.
- If two numbers are divisible by a number, then their difference will also be divisible by that number. *e.g.,* 45 and 20 both are divisible by 5. Their difference $45 - 20 = 25$ is also divisible by 5.

Measurement of Time

60	Seconds (s)	=	1	Minute (min)
60	Minutes	=	1	Hour (h)
24	Hours	=	1	Day
7	Days	=	1	Week
30	Days	=	1	Month
365	Days	=	1	Year
366	Days	=	1	Leap year
52	Weeks	=	1	Year
12	Months	=	1	Year
10	Years	=	1	Decade
100	Years	=	1	Century
1000	Years	=	1	Millennium

Leap Year

A leap year comes once in every four years. If the last two digits of an year are divisible by 4, it is a leap year. But if it is a century year like 2000, it should be divisible by 400 to be a leap year.

- A month may normally have 30 or 31 days.
- The month of February normally has 28 days but in a leap year it has 29 days.

Jubilee Celebrations:

Anniversary	=	1	Year
Decade	=	10	Years
Silver Jubilee	=	25	Years
Golden Jubilee	=	50	Years
Diamond Jubilee	=	60	Years
Platinum Jubilee	=	75	Years
Century	=	100	Years

Happenings:

Every Day	=	Daily
Every Week	=	Weekly
Every Month	=	Monthly
Twice a Month	=	Fortnightly
Every Year	=	Annually
Twice a Year	=	Half Yearly
Once in Two Years	=	Biennially

Days, Months & Years

The number of days in each month can also be found by counting across the knuckles and valleys on the back of each clenched fist (from left to right). See illustration:

All months which come on knuckles always have 31 days.

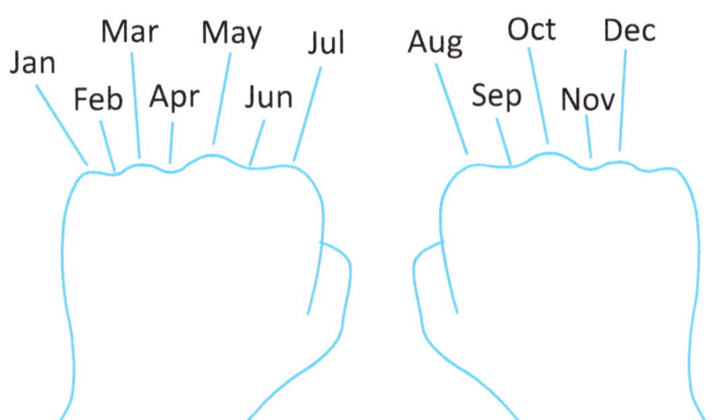

All months which come on valleys always have 30 days, except February.

AM-PM

Ante Meridiem (a.m.) denotes the time after midnight and before noon: *e.g.* 2 a.m., 6 a.m., 10.30 a.m. etc. 12 a.m. denotes midnight.

Post Meridiem (p.m.) denotes the time after noon and before midnight *e.g.* 3 p.m., 11 p.m. etc. 12 p.m. denotes noon.

Months of the Year and Days

Month	Days
January	31
February	28 or 29
March	31
April	30
May	31
June	30
July	31
August	31
September	30
October	31
November	30
December	31

AD-BC

Anno Domini (AD) denotes that the year comes after Christ's birth: *e.g.,* 2000 AD, 2017 AD.

Before Christ (BC) denotes that the year comes before Christ's birth: *e.g.,* 1000 BC, 500 BC.

- The time taken by moon to travel around earth is called a LUNAR MONTH. It is near about 29 ½ days. It is measured from one new moon to the next.
- The time earth takes to rotate once around sun is called a SOLAR YEAR. The nearest total time is 365 days, 5 hours, 48 minutes and 47½ seconds.

The Metric System

Meaning of Prefixes

Milli	=	One-thousandth part
Centi	=	One-hundreth part
Deci	=	One-tenth part
Deca	=	Ten times (10)
Hecto	=	Hundred times (100)
Kilo	=	Thousand times (1000)

Length

10	millimetres (mm)	=	1	centimetre (cm)
10	centimetres	=	1	decimetre (dm)
10	decimetres	=	1	metre (m)
10	metres	=	1	decametre (dam)
10	decametres	=	1	hectometre (hm)
10	hectometres	=	1	kilometre (km)
100	centimetres	=	1	metre (m)
1000	metres	=	1	kilometre (km)

Capacity

10	millilitres (ml)	=	1	centilitre (cl)
10	centilitres	=	1	decilitre (dl)
10	decilitres	=	1	litre (l)
1000	millilitres	=	1	litre
10	litres	=	1	decalitre (dal)
10	decalitres	=	1	hectolitre (hl)
10	hectolitres	=	1	kilolitre (kl)

- Length, Width and Height are measured mostly in centimetres and metres.
- Distance is measured mostly in metres, kilometres and miles.
- Quantity of liquids is mostly measured in millilitres, litres and kilolitres.

Weighing Measures

10	milligrams (mg)	=	1	centigram (cg)
10	centigrams	=	1	decigram (dg)
10	decigrams	=	1	gram (g)
10	grams	=	1	decagram (dag)
10	decagrams	=	1	hectogram (hg)
10	hectograms	=	1	kilogram (kg)
100	centigrams	=	1	gram (gm)
1000	grams	=	1	kilogram
100	kilograms	=	1	quintal (ql)
10	quintals	=	1	tonne (t)
1000	kilograms	=	1	tonne

Linear Customary Measures

12	inches (in)	=	1	foot (ft *or* ')
3	feet	=	1	yard (yd)
1	yard	=	36	inches (in *or* ")
5½	yards	=	1	pole, rod *or* perch
220	yards	=	1	furlong (fur)
1760	yards	=	1	mile (mi)
1	acre	=	4840	sq yard

Counting Measures

1	unit	=	1
2	units	=	1 pair
12	units	=	1 dozen
20	units	=	1 score
144	units	=	1 gross
12	dozen	=	1 gross
1728	units/12 gross	=	1 great gross

A Pair

A Dozen

Arithmetical Terms

Sum

The total resulting from addition of two or more numbers.

e.g., The sum of 20 and 30 is = 20 + 30 = 50.

$$\begin{array}{r} 20 \\ +\ 30 \\ \hline 50 \\ \hline \end{array}$$

Difference

The remainder left after subtraction of one number from another number. *e.g.,* The difference of 30 and 20 is = 30 – 20 = 10.

$$\begin{array}{r} 30 \\ -\ 20 \\ \hline 10 \\ \hline \end{array}$$

Product

A number resulting from multiplication of one number by another number. *e.g.,* The product of 100 and 2 is = 100 × 2 = 200.

$$\begin{array}{r} 100 \\ \times\ 2 \\ \hline 200 \\ \hline \end{array}$$

Quotient

A number resulting from division of one number by another number.

e.g., The quotient of 50 and 10 is = 50 ÷ 10 = 5.

10) 50 (5
50
0

Dividend

The number which is divided by another number is called dividend.

e.g., The dividend in 100 ÷ 50 is 100.

50) 100 (2
100
0

Divisor

The number which divides the dividend is called divisor.

e.g., The divisor in 500 ÷ 100 is 100.

100) 500 (5
100
0

Remainder

The number which is left undivided after the division of a number by another number.

e.g., in 10 ÷ 3 the remainder left is 1.

3) 10 (3
9
1

Mathematical Symbols

Name	Symbol
Plus (Addition)	$+$
Division	$\div$
Greater than	$>$
Less than	$<$
Per cent	%
Triangle	$\triangle$
Parallel to	$\parallel$
Implies	$\Rightarrow$
Since	$\because$
Is as	$::$
Function	f
Integers	Z or I
Union	$\cup$
Set	{: :}

Name	Symbol
Minus (Subtraction)	$-$
Equal to	$=$
Not greater than	$\ngtr$
Not less than	$\nless$
Angle	$\angle$
Square	$\square$
Rectangle	▭
Implies and Implied by	$\Leftarrow$
Decimal	$\cdot$
Plus or Minus	$\pm$
Addition	Σ
Square root	$\sqrt{}$
Intersection	$\cap$
Set of natural numbers	N

Name	Symbol
Multiplication (Product)	$\times$
Not equal to	$\neq$
Greater than or Equal to	$\geq$
Less than or Equal to	$\leq$
Right angle	∟
Circle	$\bigcirc$
Perpendicular to	$\perp$
Therefore	$\therefore$
Ratio	$:$
Is approximately	$\simeq$
Inch	"
x degrees	x°
Varies as	$\propto$
Set of whole numbers	W

Squares and Cubes 1-30

Squares

If a number is multiplied once by itself, the product is called its square.
e.g., $2 \times 2 = 2^2 = 4$. Here 4 is called the square of 2.

Squares of Numbers 1 to 30

1^2	=	1	11^2	=	121	21^2	=	441
2^2	=	4	12^2	=	144	22^2	=	484
3^2	=	9	13^2	=	169	23^2	=	529
4^2	=	16	14^2	=	196	24^2	=	576
5^2	=	25	15^2	=	225	25^2	=	625
6^2	=	36	16^2	=	256	26^2	=	676
7^2	=	49	17^2	=	289	27^2	=	729
8^2	=	64	18^2	=	324	28^2	=	784
9^2	=	81	19^2	=	361	29^2	=	841
10^2	=	100	20^2	=	400	30^2	=	900

Cubes

If a number is multiplied twice by itself, the product is called its cube.
e.g., $2 \times 2 \times 2 = 2^3 = 8$. Here 8 is called the cube of 2.

Cubes of Numbers 1 to 30

1^3	=	1	11^3	=	1331	21^3	=	9261
2^3	=	8	12^3	=	1728	22^3	=	10648
3^3	=	27	13^3	=	2197	23^3	=	12167
4^3	=	64	14^3	=	2744	24^3	=	13824
5^3	=	125	15^3	=	3375	25^3	=	15625
6^3	=	216	16^3	=	4096	26^3	=	17576
7^3	=	343	17^3	=	4913	27^3	=	19683
8^3	=	512	18^3	=	5832	28^3	=	21952
9^3	=	729	19^3	=	6859	29^3	=	24389
10^3	=	1000	20^3	=	8000	30^3	=	27000

The Numeration System

Hindu-Arabic (Indian) System

Unit	1
Ten	10
Hundred	100
Thousand	1,000
Ten Thousand	10,000
Lakh	1,00,000
Ten Lakh	10,00,000
Crore	1,00,00,000
Ten Crore	10,00,00,000
Arab	1,00,00,00,000
Ten Arab	10,00,00,00,000
Kharab	1,00,00,00,00,000
Ten Kharab	10,00,00,00,00,000

International System

Unit	1
Ten	10
Hundred	100
Thousand	1,000
Ten Thousand	10,000
Hundred Thousand	100,000
Million	1,000,000
Ten Million	10,000,000
Hundred Million	100,000,000
Billion	1,000,000,000
Ten Billion	10,000,000,000
Hundred Billion	100,000,000,000
Trillion	1,000,000,000,000

Roman System

Unit	I
Five	V
Ten	X
Fifty	L
Hundred	C
Five Hundred	D
One Thousand	M
Five Thousand	$\overline{V}$
Ten Thousand	$\overline{X}$
Hundred Thousand	$\overline{C}$

Devanagari Numbers

One	१
Two	२
Three	३
Four	४
Five	५
Six	६
Seven	७
Eight	८
Nine	९
Ten	१०

English Ordinals

1st	First
2nd	Second
3rd	Third
4th	Fourth
5th	Fifth
6th	Sixth
7th	Seventh
8th	Eighth
9th	Ninth
10th	Tenth

- Terms like Lakh, Crore, Arab and Kharab are used in Indian System only.
- Terms like Million, Billion and Trillion are used in International System.

Indian Currency

 The new symbol of Indian currency is ₹ which is derived from the Devanagari consonant 'र' (Ra) with an added horizontal bar. It had been approved on 15 July, 2010 and was designed by IIT Mumbai Post-graduate D. Udaya Kumar. Earlier Rupee was denoted as 'Re' or 'Rs'.

₹ 1 ₹ 2 ₹ 5 ₹ 10 ₹ 20 ₹ 50 ₹ 100

www.ingramcontent.com/pod-product-compliance
Ingram Content Group UK Ltd.
Pitfield, Milton Keynes, MK11 3LW, UK
UKHW062002290726
14090UKWH00021B/1339